The Ocean Fairies

For Natilla Leigh Anderson, a true
friend of the fairies!

Special thanks
to Sue Mongredien

ORCHARD BOOKS
338 Euston Road, London NW1 3BH
Orchard Books Australia
Level 17/207 Kent Street, Sydney, NSW 2000
A Paperback Original

First published in 2010 by Orchard Books

Illustrations © Orchard Books 2010

A CIP catalogue record for this book is available
from the British Library.

ISBN 978 1 40830 819 6
5 7 9 10 8 6

Printed in Great Britain

The paper and board used in this paperback are natural recyclable
products made from wood grown in sustainable forests. The
manufacturing processes conform to the environmental regulations
of the country of origin.

Orchard Books is a division of Hachette Children's Books,
an Hachette UK company

www.hachette.co.uk

Stephanie
the Starfish
Fairy

by Daisy Meadows

ORCHARD BOOKS

www.rainbowmagic.co.uk

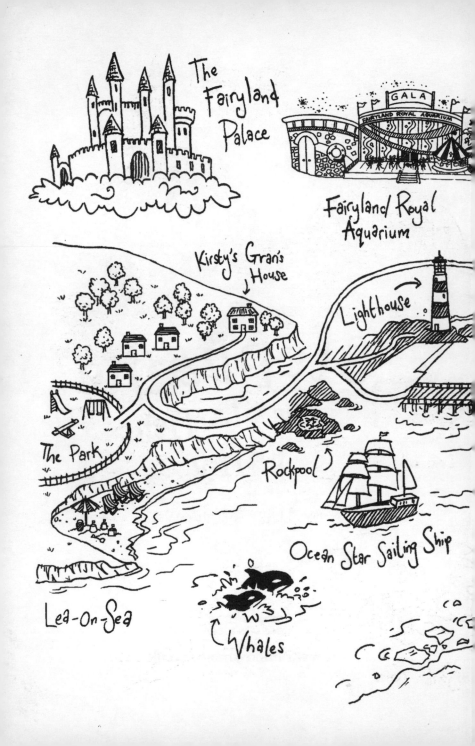

The
Fairyland
Palace

Fairyland Royal
Aquarium

GALA

FAIRYLAND ROYAL AQUARIUM

Kirsty's Gran's
House

Lighthouse

The Park

Rockpool

Ocean Star Sailing Ship

Lea-On-Sea

Whales

The Magical Conch Shell at my side,
I'll rule the oceans far and wide!
But my foolish goblins have shattered the shell,
So now I cast my icy spell.

Seven shell fragments, be gone, I say,
To the human world to hide away,
Now the shell is gone, it's plain to see,
The oceans will never have harmony!

Contents

Starry Skies

"The sea sounds so much louder at night, doesn't it?" Kirsty Tate said to her best friend Rachel Walker as they made their way down to Leamouth beach in darkness. The stars twinkled in the sky above them, and there was a full moon which cast silvery streaks on the tops of the waves.

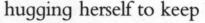

"It feels completely different down here," Rachel agreed. "No noisy seagulls, no ice-cream van, no families making sandcastles…"

Kirsty smiled. "It's exciting," she said, hugging herself to keep warm as a cool breeze swept in from the sea. "Just like everything else about this holiday, really!"

Both girls were staying with Kirsty's gran for a week of the spring holidays, and Kirsty wasn't exaggerating when she said they'd been having an exciting time.

The two friends had been helping the Ocean Fairies look for the seven missing pieces of a magical golden conch shell which had been smashed by mean Jack Frost. So far, they'd found four pieces of the shell and had four wonderful fairy adventures, but there were still three pieces left to find.

Tonight they'd been invited to join Gran's Astronomy Club for an evening picnic on the beach. The forecast was for a beautifully clear night, so Gran and her friends had brought down trestle tables and picnic hampers to the beach, as well as some impressive-looking telescopes, too.

Kirsty and Rachel helped set the food out as the guests arrived and then, as the sky grew darker still, Gran showed them some of the constellations. "There are eighty-eight constellations – or 'groups of stars'," she told the girls, and pointed upwards. "There's an easy one – the Great Bear or, as we used to call it when I was a girl, the Saucepan. Do you see the shape of a saucepan up there?"

Rachel and Kirsty stared at where she was pointing. "Yes!"

Rachel cried excitedly. "I see it. There's a handle, and there's the pan."

"Oh yes!" Kirsty said, gazing up. "Well, the 'saucepan' is part of the Great Bear," Gran explained. "The handle is the bear's tail, and the 'pan' is part of the bear's body. If you look carefully, you can see legs and a head shape, too." She smiled at the girls through the darkness. "It's a bit like joining up the dots to make a picture."

While Gran passed around cups of coffee from her thermos, Kirsty and Rachel continued to stare at the stars, trying to spot more pictures. "I can see a violin shape," Rachel said, showing Kirsty. "It's just like Victoria the Violin Fairy's."

"Oh yes," Kirsty said. "And there's a shoe shape, with ribbons attached, like Ruby the Red Fairy's shoe!"

An excited clamour went up amongst the Astronomy Club members at that moment, and the girls saw that some of them were pointing at the sky. "A shooting star!" Gran exclaimed. "Well, I never. That's very special. Make a wish, girls!"

"I wish we could meet another Ocean Fairy soon," Rachel murmured at once.

Kirsty heard her. "That's what I wished for too," she whispered. "We *must* find the other pieces of the Magical Golden Conch Shell. We've only got two days left here in Leamouth and there are still three pieces missing!"

The Magical Golden Conch Shell was very important. Every year at a grand ocean-side gala, Shannon the Ocean Fairy would play a special tune on the shell, and this would ensure order throughout the world's oceans. Before she'd been able to play the tune this year, though, Jack Frost had sent his goblin servants to snatch the conch shell from her. He said he hated the seaside as it was far too warm and noisy and he didn't see why anyone else should have fun there.

Unfortunately the goblins had begun fighting over who got to carry the shell and then dropped it, smashing it into seven pieces as they did so. The Ocean Fairies had all tried to grab the broken pieces, but before they could reach them, Jack Frost had cast a spell, sending the shattered shell fragments into the human world, before vanishing.

The Fairy Queen had used her magic
to send the Ocean Fairies' special animal
helpers out into the oceans to each guard
a piece of the broken conch shell. Kirsty
and Rachel had been helping the Ocean
Fairies find their animal friends, who had
led them each time to another piece of the
shell. But Jack Frost's sneaky goblins were
looking for the shell pieces too – and were
desperate to please their master by finding
them first.

Down fell the shooting star now,
past the constellations that looked like
Victoria's violin and Ruby's shoe. "Here,
girls," came a voice just then. It was one
of Gran's friends, a nice old man called
Frank. "Would you like to watch the
shooting star through this telescope? You'll
be able to see it more clearly."

"Yes, please," said Rachel, putting her eye to the telescope. Then she stiffened with excitement as she saw the shooting star, now magnified. Only…it wasn't actually a shooting star at all. It was Stephanie the Starfish Fairy!

Trapped!

"Kirsty, have a look," Rachel said meaningfully, trying her hardest not to show how delighted she was in front of the astronomers.

Kirsty took the telescope and peered through...then gasped as she saw what Rachel had noticed. There was Stephanie,

her short red hair blowing in the wind as
she flew. She wore a funky grey jumpsuit,
a denim waistcoat
and wedge-heeled
sandals, and was
heading for a
group of rock
pools further
up the beach,
her tiny body
glowing in the
darkness. Was that to
alert the girls that she was there? Kirsty
wondered with a shiver of excitement.

Rachel was smiling to herself too. She
was sure Stephanie had come to the beach
to look for her starfish, Spike – which
hopefully meant another piece of the
magical shell would be nearby!

"Thank you," Kirsty said politely to
Frank, moving away from the telescope.
"She – I mean *it* – looks wonderful
close-up."

The bright light of Stephanie suddenly
vanished as it plunged to earth, and the
grown-ups turned back to their picnic.

"I think we should investigate," Kirsty
murmured to Rachel. "Come on, let's ask
my gran if we can have a look around."

Kirsty's gran was tucking into a plate of
sandwiches.
"Of course you
can have a
wander," she
said, when the
girls went
over and
asked her.

"You've both got torches, haven't you? Just tread carefully, the seaweed might be slippery, and stay away from the water's edge. And don't go too far."

"We won't," Rachel promised as they hurried away, shining their torchlights along the beach. "I wonder where Stephanie is," she said to Kirsty, once they were a safe distance from the grown-ups. A cloud had slipped over the moon, making the beach seem much darker now.

The girls shone their torches across the sand and rocks, but could see no sign of the little fairy.

"I hope she didn't fall *in* one of the rock pools," Kirsty said anxiously. "She'd be in trouble if her wings got soggy – she wouldn't be able to fly!"

She and Rachel were just starting to worry when suddenly Stephanie's sparkly light reappeared. "Oh, there she is," Rachel hissed excitedly. "Why is she shining like that though, I wonder?"

The two friends stared as they saw the little fairy's bright light zipping about frantically in all directions. "I think she's just letting us know where she is," Kirsty replied. "Come on, let's shine our torches over there so we can see her better."

She and Rachel both held out their torches and angled them so that the lights fell on Stephanie.

But then, with a lurch of dismay, they realised why the fairy was thrashing around. She'd been caught in a rock pooling net…which was held by a goblin!

"Oh no," Rachel whispered. "Come on, we've got to help her!"

They ran towards Stephanie and the goblin but soon saw that he wasn't alone. There were *three* goblins dressed in black with brown camouflage stripes across their faces, which made them even harder to see in the dark.

"What are those lights?" one of the
goblins asked, blinking as the torchbeams
shone on his face. "I can't see with them
in my eyes."

"Turn away from them then, you nit,"
another goblin snapped. "And hurry up
and tie that net before the fairy escapes."

"Help!" cried Stephanie, still fighting to
get out. "Help me!"

The girls rushed forwards but they were too late. One of the goblins used a long piece of seaweed to tie up the top of the net…and then Stephanie was trapped!

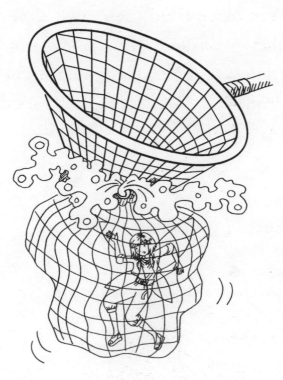

Searching for Spike

Shocked and alarmed, Rachel and Kirsty turned off their torches and ducked down behind the rocks, out of sight. There was just enough light from Stephanie for them to see the goblins carrying the net around the rock pools, holding it above the water and peering down. "She is the *star*fish fairy, I suppose," Kirsty thought aloud. "Maybe she always shines like a star?"

"Yes, and now the goblins are using her light to help them hunt for Spike, I bet," Rachel realised, her heart thumping. It was horrible to see poor Stephanie swinging around so helplessly in the net.

"We've got to get her out of there," Kirsty muttered, "and somehow find Spike before the goblins do. Let me think…"

Before the girls could come up with a good plan, though, they both noticed a pink sparkly light appear from a nearby pool. "Aha!

That must be the starfish!" cheered the goblins, rushing over.

Rachel felt tense as she watched them searching. "Where is it?" the goblins grumbled. "Stupid starfish, we saw you sparkling, we know you're there somewhere!"

"There's nothing there," one of them muttered crossly after they'd splashed around for a while. "We must have got it wrong."

"There's a different sparkly light!" another goblin called, sounding more cheerful. "Maybe *that's* the starfish."

The goblins rushed over to another pool where Kirsty and Rachel could see another faint shimmering from the water. But as soon as the goblins reached the pool, the light vanished.

"I wonder if that really *is* Spike," Kirsty whispered to Rachel as the goblins hunted in vain. "I'm starting to think it might be clever Stephanie, magicking up those lights to fool the goblins!"

Rachel nodded. "I bet you're right," she said. "Good old Stephanie. And while she's keeping them busy running around after the different lights, we should try to find Spike ourselves. Where shall we look first?"

"Hmmm," said Kirsty. "Well, my guess is that Stephanie was heading straight for Spike before she was caught." She gazed up at the stars. "She went past the violin shape, didn't she? And then past Ruby's red shoe..." She paused, staring in surprise. "I don't remember *that* constellation, do you?"

Rachel looked up at the pattern of stars Kirsty had seen next to the shoe. "Your gran said it was like joining the dots, didn't she?" she said, trying to work out the picture in this new constellation. Then she gave a squeak of excitement as she realised what it was. "A starfish! It's a clue!"

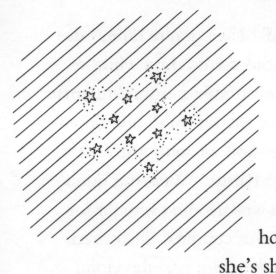

Kirsty grinned. "Stephanie must have used her fairy magic to make it," she said happily. "And she's showing us where she thinks Spike is – and hopefully another piece of the conch shell. Let's go!"

The girls crept over to the rock pool directly under the starfish constellation. They had to go quietly so that the goblins didn't see or hear them. Thankfully, the goblins had been led to yet another sparkly light in the opposite direction, so they were busily splashing about there, moaning about how much they hated getting wet.

As Kirsty and Rachel reached the rock
pool, the moon slid out from behind the
clouds again, and suddenly it was much
easier to see what they were doing. There
were mussel shells and barnacles around
the edge of the pool and…hooray! Right
at the edge of the shallow water, pulsing
with a faint pink light, was a starfish.
"Ooh," Rachel whispered excitedly.
"Spike, is that you?"

Rock Pool Discoveries

Both girls peered at the pinky-yellow starfish that lay in the pool, then grinned as it lifted up one arm and gave them a little wave.

"So it *is* you, Spike," Kirsty said happily. "Excellent!" She put a hand in the pool to pick him up and Spike hopped into her palm. "I wonder where the shell is? Have you been guarding it, Spike?"

Previously, when they'd found the magical ocean creatures, the animals had been able to talk to their fairy mistresses, and the girls had been able to understand them, but if Spike was trying to speak to them now, they couldn't hear a sound. He was wriggling on Kirsty's hand as if he could hear *her* though.

"Do you think he's trying to tell us something?" Rachel wondered.

"It must be because Stephanie isn't here that we can't hear him," Kirsty replied.

Just then, Rachel caught a glimpse of something golden hidden under a seaweed plant in the rock pool. "Ooh," she said, lifting the seaweed at once. "It's the shell!"

The mussels began opening and closing their own shells as if they were applauding and Spike seemed to dance a jig for joy on Kirsty's hand.

Rachel beamed as she scooped up the golden piece of conch shell – the fifth piece they'd found!

"Brilliant," Kirsty said happily. "So we've found Spike *and* the shell… Now we just need to rescue Stephanie so she can take them both back to Fairyland." She and Rachel glanced over to where Stephanie was still using her fairy magic to cast sparkles in the pools to trick the goblins. "The lights she's making look fainter to me," Rachel said anxiously.

"Oh dear — she must be very tired by now, with all the magic she's used," Kirsty said. "What should we do?"

Rachel thought for a moment. The goblins sounded more and more bad-tempered as they went on hunting for Spike, and they might turn even nastier if she and Kirsty tried to rescue Stephanie. If only they had someone to help them!

Then an idea struck her. "We could use our lockets to go to Fairyland and ask for help," she suggested, grabbing the pretty locket she wore around her neck.

The Fairy King and Queen had given
one each to Rachel and Kirsty, and they
contained fairy dust that would take them
to Fairyland.

"Good idea," Kirsty said, opening
her locket and sprinkling fairy dust over
herself. She sprinkled some of the glittering
dust over Spike, too, and then she and
Rachel held hands, waiting for the sparkly
whirlwind to whisk them all away to
Fairyland as it usually did.

But nothing happened. "That's strange," Rachel said. "Does it only work in daylight or something?"

"Maybe we didn't use enough," Kirsty said, sprinkling another pinch of dust over herself. But still nothing happened.

Spike squirmed on her hand and Kirsty glanced down at him. "I wonder if it's because Spike's not with his fairy mistress?" she said to Rachel. "Perhaps the magic won't let us take him or the shell without Stephanie."

45

She bit her lip. "Looks like we'll have to leave them both behind while we get help."

"Let's hide you very carefully then, Spike," Rachel said, as Kirsty lowered him back into the pool. "And we'll hide the piece of shell too."

The girls tucked Spike and the golden piece of conch into a group of anemones. The anemones were the exact same shade of pink as Spike,

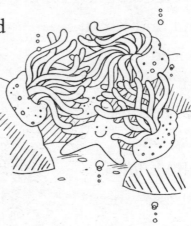

and their waving fronds closed around him, almost as if they knew they had to keep him and the shell out of sight.

The moment the girls had finished, a whirlwind spangled with twinkling stars whipped up around them. They were off to Fairyland!

Shannon to the Rescue

A few seconds later, Rachel and Kirsty felt themselves being lowered gently to the ground, and the whirlwind vanished. They looked around to see that they were in Fairyland, and that the whirlwind had brought them to the Royal Aquarium where their Ocean Fairy adventures had begun.

Sitting outside the Aquarium was
Shannon the Ocean Fairy herself, her
wings drooping sadly. She jumped up,
looking more cheerful when she saw
the girls nearby. "Oh, hello!" she called.
"Have you found
another piece
of the Golden
Conch?"

"Yes,
we have,"
Rachel
replied, "*and*
we've found
Spike…but there's
a problem."

She and Kirsty went on to explain
how Stephanie had been captured by the
goblins and was being held prisoner in

their fishing net. "And Stephanie seems
really tired now, and we're worried about
her," Kirsty finished. "Will you help us
rescue her?"

Shannon nodded. "Of course," she
replied. "Let's go to Leamouth!"

She waved her wand and a whirlwind appeared, pulling the three of them up into the air, spinning faster and faster until everything was a blur of rainbow colours and glitter. Moments later, they were back in Leamouth – but Kirsty and Rachel weren't their usual human selves any more. Shannon had turned them into fairies, and they each had beautiful sparkling wings on their backs.

"Down here," Shannon called, darting behind a large rock. "Oh!" she cried in surprise.

Kirsty and Rachel fluttered quickly
after her, wondering what she'd found.
"Puffins!" exclaimed Rachel in delight as
she recognised the comical-looking black
and white birds who were already behind
the rock. "I've never seen a real one
before!"

Shannon frowned. "I've certainly never

seen them at *night* before," she replied,
before flying up to the biggest puffin.
"Guys, you're supposed to be asleep now,
not wandering around on the beach!" She
shook her head. "This is because
the Golden Conch Shell
is still broken," she
told Rachel
and Kirsty.
"The ocean
creatures
are in such
a muddle.
The sooner
we can fix the
shell and I can
play the ocean
tune on it,
the better."

Kirsty glanced around for the goblins. "There they are," she said, spotting them nearby. "And there's Stephanie in the net, can you see?"

The silvery moon above them cast just enough light to show poor Stephanie lying at the bottom of the net.

"Oh dear," Shannon said. "I'm so glad you came to me for help, girls. She does need rescuing – and fast. Let me think…"

Her pretty face scrunched into a frown
as she tried to come up with a plan.
Rachel and Kirsty thought hard too, but it
was difficult to concentrate with the puffin
family shuffling around, pecking at the
seaweed and making soft squawking noises
to each other.

Then Shannon grinned. "It's lucky that the puffins are here, actually. They might just be able to help us out."

"What do you mean?" Rachel asked.

"I mean, let's set a trap," Shannon said, still smiling. "And we'll get the ocean creatures to join in. If we all work together, I'm sure we can stop those goblins!"

Super Stars!

A few minutes later, Kirsty, Rachel and Shannon had everything in place. "So I'll use my magic to make a pink glow in this rock pool so that the goblins think I'm Spike..." Shannon reminded the girls.

"And we'll try to tempt them over," Kirsty giggled. "Aren't they in for a nice surprise?"

She and Rachel fluttered through the darkness to where the goblins were crossly searching through yet another rock pool for Spike. "I think we've already gone through this pool," one of them was complaining. "And I'm fed up! If I have to touch one more slimy piece of seaweed, I'll…"

"Hello there, having fun?" Rachel asked sweetly as she and Kirsty hovered in mid-air above their heads.

"You!" the goblin snarled, his eyes gleaming furiously. "What are you doing here? Don't you know what happens to meddling fairies? We catch 'em!" He held up the net with Stephanie inside it warningly.

"Ahh, but we can *help* you," Kirsty said. "We know where the magic starfish *and* the piece of conch shell are. And we'll tell you, if you like."

"The only thing is," Rachel added, "we need you to give us our friend in exchange. Do we have a deal?"

The goblins scoffed at this. "Yeah, right," the tallest one said, scowling. "We're not falling for your stupid tricks. You can have this fairy back *after* we've found the shell piece and not before."

Just then, his friend elbowed him. "Hey, look!" he said, pointing to the rock pool where Shannon was hiding. A bright pink light was streaming from it. He turned back to the fairies with a jeering look. "Ha! We don't need your deals," he said. "We can find the starfish and shell all by ourselves!"

And with that, they rushed gleefully towards the glowing rock pool.

Kirsty put two fingers between her lips and blew a piercing whistle. That was the signal for the fun to start!

As the goblins ran across the sand, they were suddenly set upon by the puffin family, who flew at them, squawking and snapping their great beaks. The goblins were terrified!

"Help! It's a bird monster!" one of them yelped, trying to dodge the puffin who was nipping at his ankle. "Run faster!"

Swerving and stumbling, the goblins finally made it past the puffins – but moments later, they were set upon by a whole horde of crabs who jabbed at the goblins' legs with their sharp pincers. "Ow! Ow! Ow! What's going on?" the goblins cried in fright. "The beach is full of monsters!"

Two of the goblins managed to get
away, but a large
red crab had a
tight hold of
the other
goblin's big
toe and was
pinching it for
all he was worth.
This goblin had to sit
down and try to wrestle the crab off.

"That's stopped one of them..." Kirsty
said, watching in glee. "The plan's
working brilliantly!"

Next, the goblins had to clamber over
some other rock pools to get to where
Shannon was. But in his haste, one of the
goblins tripped over a large lumpy rock,
and fell, smack onto the seaweed.

Before he could move, the crowd of puffins had rushed up to him and circled him. Then they began pecking at him all over again. "Ow!" he cried. "Go away! Shoo!"

"That's two down…" Rachel said, smiling as the puffins showed no sign of letting the goblin go anywhere. "And the goblin who's left is the one with Stephanie. Let's hope the last part of the plan works…"

The goblin with the net began
clambering around the next rock pool,
still intent on finding Spike and the conch
piece. But Shannon had asked the ocean
snails and sea sponges to make the rocks
around this pool extra slippery, and the
goblin soon found it very difficult to keep
his balance.

"Whooooaaa!" he cried, skidding and
sliding, his arms waving in the air.

"Heeelllppp!"

On his very next step, he skidded right into the rock pool – and the net went flying out of his grasp. "Yuck!" he wailed as he splashed into the water. "I'm covered in smelly seaweed!"

Meanwhile, Rachel and Kirsty went diving to catch the net, and so did Shannon, flying out of her hiding place in the last rock pool. Between the three of them, they took hold of it, and lowered it gently to the ground.

Then they untied the top of the net and Stephanie fluttered out, looking pale and tired, but relieved to be freed. "Thank you, all of you," she said,

hugging them each in turn. "It's so good to be out of that horrible net!"

"We've found Spike and the piece of conch," Rachel told her excitedly. "Come and see!"

They led Stephanie over to the pool where the anemones were still hiding Spike and the shell from sight. As soon as he saw his fairy mistress, Spike gave a happy wriggle all over. "*There* you are!" he said.

Stephanie touched Spike with her wand and he shrank down to fairy-size and leapt into her arms. Then Shannon waved *her* wand over Kirsty and Rachel, who turned back into girls again.

"Thank you so much," she smiled. "I'm delighted that we've got another piece of the Conch Shell. Stephanie and I will shrink this and take it back to Fairyland."

"Goodbye and thanks again," Stephanie said. "Oh, and enjoy the stars!"

And with a last flurry of fairy dust, she, Spike and Shannon were gone.

"Enjoy the stars?" Rachel echoed as she and Kirsty made their way back towards Gran and her friends. "What did she mean by that?"

"She must have known we were here with the Astronomy Club, I guess," Kirsty replied. "Look, there's Gran now. Hello!" she called, as they reached the group of people.

Kirsty's gran was offering around a tray of biscuits and she smiled at the girls. "Just in time for a biscuit," she said. "Take a few each, there's plenty."

The biscuits were cut in all different shapes and sizes, and Kirsty smiled as she saw that several were star-shaped.

Remembering Stephanie's words, Kirsty
deliberately took a star-shaped biscuit,
and so did Rachel.

"Just like the shooting star," Gran
chuckled. "I hope your wishes come
true, girls."

Kirsty and Rachel
smiled at each other
as Gran bustled
away. "They
already *did*
come true,"
Rachel said.
Kirsty bit
into her biscuit.
"Yum," she
said. "And now
I'm *definitely* going to
enjoy these stars!"

RAINBOW magic

The Ocean Fairies

Stephanie the Starfish Fairy has
found her piece of the Golden Conch
Shell! Now Rachel and Kirsty
must help...

Whitney the Whale Fairy

All Aboard the Ocean Star

"This is brilliant fun, Kirsty!" Rachel Walker called to her best friend, Kirsty Tate, as their ship, the *Ocean Star*, bobbed across the waves. "Look, can you see that shoal of fish?"

Kirsty peered over the ship's rail and saw the tiny, silvery fish darting through the sparkling turquoise water. Some of the other girls and boys on the boat trip rushed over to look, too.

"Leamouth looks so lovely in the sunshine, doesn't it?" Kirsty remarked, as they sailed across the bay. She and Rachel stood on the deck of the *Ocean*

Star, enjoying the view of the pretty
seaside resort with its golden beach and
whitewashed cottages clustered around
the harbour.

Kirsty and Rachel were spending
the spring holiday in Leamouth with
Kirsty's gran. Gran had suggested
that today the girls took a special trip
just for children on an old-fashioned
sailing ship, run by Captain Andy
and his crew. Rachel and Kirsty were
fascinated by the large wooden boat
with its tall masts and huge, billowing,
white sails.

"Ahoy there, sailors!" Captain
Andy shouted, waving at the girls and
boys on the deck below him. He was
standing behind the wooden ship's
wheel, turning it to and fro to guide the

boat along. "If you'd visited Leamouth hundreds of years ago, the harbour would have been full of large sailing ships just like the *Ocean Star*. There was one very famous boat called the *Mermaid*, but sadly it sank somewhere around this area a very long time ago."

"Do you know where the wreck is, Captain Andy?" asked Thomas, one of the boys on the trip.

Captain Andy shook his head. "No-one knows exactly where the ship sank," he replied. "The ship had a beautiful carved and painted figure of a mermaid attached to its front. The legend says that the mermaid statue now watches over this area from wherever the wreck lies on the bed of the ocean."

"What a great story," Rachel remarked to Kirsty. "It sounds like magic!"

"And we know all about *that*, don't we, Rachel?" Kirsty whispered, winking at her friend.

The two girls were right in the middle of another thrilling fairy adventure. When they'd arrived in Leamouth, they'd received an invitation to visit the Fairyland Ocean Gala, where they'd met their old friend Shannon the Ocean Fairy. Rachel and Kirsty had also been introduced to Shannon's helpers, the seven Ocean Fairies, and their Magical Ocean Creatures, who lived in the Royal Aquarium...

The Ocean Fairies

Win Rainbow Magic goodies!

In every book in the Ocean Fairies series
(books 85-91) there is a hidden picture of a shell with a
letter in it. Find all seven letters and re-arrange them to
make a special Ocean Fairies word, then send it to us.
Each month we will put the entries into a draw and select
one winner to receive a Rainbow Magic sparkly T-shirt
and goody bag!

Send your entry on a postcard to Rainbow Magic Ocean
Fairies Competition, Orchard Books, 338 Euston Road,
London NW1 3BH. Australian readers should write to
Hachette Children's Books, Level 17/207 Kent Street,
Sydney, NSW 2000.
New Zealand readers should write to Rainbow Magic
Competition, 4 Whetu Place, Mairangi Bay, Auckland,
NZ. Don't forget to include your name and address.
Only one entry per child.
Final draw: 30th April 2011.

Have you checked out the

website at:
www.rainbowmagic.co.uk

Meet the Twilight Fairies

in September 2010!

Ava the Sunset Fairy
978-1-40830-906-3

Lexi the Firefly Fairy
978-1-40830-907-0

Zara the Starlight Fairy
978-1-40830-908-7

Morgan the Midnight Fairy
978-1-40830-909-4

Yasmin the Night Owl Fairy
978-1-40830-910-0

Maisie the Moonbeam Fairy
978-1-40830-911-7

Sabrina the Sweet Dreams Fairy
978-1-40830-912-4